PRO...
OF...
FARGO PUBLIC LIBRARY

W9-CVA-308

I'll Be the Horse
If You'll Play With Me

STORY AND PICTURES BY
Martha Alexander

The Dial Press / New York

JP

c.7.

Copyright © 1975 by Martha Alexander / All rights reserved
First Printing / Printed in the United States of America

Library of Congress Cataloging in Publication Data
Alexander, Martha G. I'll be the horse if you'll play with me.
[1. Brothers and sisters—Fiction. 2. Play—Fiction] I. Title.
PZ7.A3777Ij   [E]   75-9207
ISBN 0-8037-5458-2   ISBN 0-8037-5511-2 lib. bdg.

MAIN LIBRARY
CHILDRENS DEPT.
FARGO PUBLIC LIBRARY

For Christina,
Leslie, Willie, Lisa,
and Scott

"Please, Bonnie, just one more time."

"You always say that, Oliver.
Just once more."

"All right, Bonnie, I'll go play with Ira."

"I *never* get my turn.

Hello, Rufus. Let's play horse and wagon.

You can be the horse.

Rufus, you're supposed to *walk*.

I give up."

"Bonnie, you can play with me now
if you want to.

If you let me use your crayons."

"They're new. I haven't even used them yet.

You used up all my paper."

"I'm tired of drawing anyway.
Let's play cops and robbers."

"Why do *I* always have to be the robber?
I don't like being tied up."

"I quit. I don't want to play with
a crybaby."

"I don't want to play with you either.
You're too *bossy*."

"Hi, Bonnie, do you want to play fifty-two pickup?"
"Sure, Willy."

"It's easy. Fifty-two cards.
You pick them up!"

"Hello, Midnight. Will you play with me?
You can be the baby.

What a nice baby you are!

What's the matter? Did you want to
be the mother?

Oliver, do you and David want to play
with my toys and me?"
"Who wants to play with a baby sister?
Go play with Scott."

"Who wants to play with a baby *brother*?

Why, Scott, I didn't know you could
pull that wagon."

"Scott big boy!"

MAIN LIBRARY
CHILDRENS DEPT
FARGO PUBLIC LIBRARY